Bill the Warthog MYSTERIES

the BOGUS MIND MACHINE

LEGACY PRESS®
www.LegacyExpress.com

Read more about your favorite tusked detective
in these Bill the Warthog Mysteries:

Book 1
Full Metal Trench Coat

Book 2
Guarding the Tablets of Stone

Book 3
Attack of the Mutant Fruit

Book 4
Quest for the Temple of Truth

Book 5
The Bogus Mind Machine

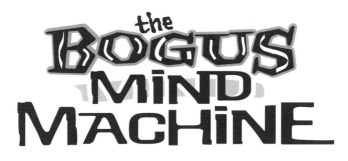

Dean A. Anderson

To Mindy, my love, the best hat in the world. As Proverbs 12:4 says, "A wife of noble character is her husband's crown."

And to my brother, Dale. Bill would be pleased with Dale's work to preserve animals in the wild through Project Survival, Cat Conservation Group, and its Sierra Endangered Cat Haven in California.

And to Sir Arthur Conan Doyle, G. K. Chesterton and Donald Sobel, Bill's literary fathers.

BILL THE WARTHOG MYSTERIES: THE BOGUS MIND MACHINE
©2010 by Dean Anderson, second printing
ISBN 10: 1-58411-080-5
ISBN 13: 978-1-58411-080-4
Legacy reorder# LP48305
JUVENILE FICTION / Religious / Christian

Legacy Press
P.O. Box 261129
San Diego, CA 92196
www.LegacyExpress.com

Mixed Sources
Product group from well-managed forests
and other controlled sources
www.fsc.org   Cert no. GFA-COC-001990
©1996 Forest Stewardship Council

Cover and Interior Illustrator: Dave Carleson

Scriptures are from the *Holy Bible: New International Version* (North American Edition), ©1973, 1978, 1984 by the International Bible Society. Used by permission of Zondervan Bible Publishers.

Printed in the United States of America

Table of Contents

Chapter 1

The Case of the Newspaper Boy

"So, Mr. Warthog, you're a real warthog; that's not a costume? How did you learn to talk? Do you have to brush your tusks? I'm sorry, as a reporter I ask a lot of questions."

"That's all right. As a detective, I ask a lot of questions as well, Mr. Foster," Bill said. "And you can call me Bill."

"You can call me Kayne."

How rude of me. Bill and Kayne have introduced themselves, but I haven't introduced you to anyone. Guess I'd better do that now.

Bill is my good friend: Bill the Warthog, private detective. We met a while ago when I hired him to solve a case for me. Afterward, he asked me to help him with his business.

You might be wondering the same thing as Kayne: is Bill really a warthog?

In fact, he is.

You see, Bill was raised in a human family, by the Thompsons, who removed him from a zoo because the zookeepers were mistreating him.

Bill grew up reading detective stories about Sherlock Holmes and Father Brown, and decided he wanted to be a detective like them. And to be a detective, Bill had to be able to talk human, walk human and wear human clothes.

As for Kayne Chas. Foster, here's what I know about him. He is about my age, in the sixth grade, but he doesn't go to Elm Street Elementary like I do. He goes to some private school that you usually need a lot of money to go to, unless you get scholarships.

Kayne doesn't get scholarships. His family is the richest in the area, maybe in the whole state.

Bill had gotten a call from Kayne asking for help with his newspaper. Not his newspaper route or his school newspaper. Kayne called us to help with the local newspaper that his parents bought for him.

I usually ask for video games for my birthday and Christmas, or if I'm feeling practical, shoes. I got skis once, and another time a bike.

Kayne's parents bought him a newspaper called the *Weekly Tribune* that goes out to thousands of people. The newspaper has ten grown-ups on the staff and printing presses and a library that has each of the weekly papers they put out over the last forty years.

Oh, I haven't told you who I am. Kayne was wondering about that too, so I'll let him ask for you.

"Who is this with you, Bill?"

"This is my friend, Nick Sayga. He is my assistant, my Watson, if you will," Bill said. "You might hear him called 'Ten Toes' because of a knack he has for playing video games with his feet."

"I've tried to type on the computer that way," Kayne said. "But people aren't interested in reading articles about SRLKAS or wenogoius, which is the stuff that comes out when I type with my feet."

"Why exactly did you call us?" Bill asked.

"Yes," Kayne said, "we should get to that. I've been looking to build up the circulation of the newspaper. I want to get more people reading the *Tribune*.

"Most people read this paper to get the local sports

scores and the police reports. A few read it to get the reports from the city council meetings. I've got an idea to get more people reading.

"I am offering a $50,000 reward for the most unusual story submitted. The most incredible, bizarre but true story brought to us gets the prize."

"Have you really thought this through?" Bill asked. "You'll attract every liar, lunatic and con man in the county with that offer!"

"That's exactly why I called you," Kayne said. "I want you to investigate every suspicious story, and I will pay you well to do so."

"I think we could do business," Bill said.

"Perhaps," Kayne said. "First, I'll need to find out if you really have a detective's mind. I'm going give you a puzzle, and we'll see if you can solve it."

"Fair enough," Bill said.

"I'm going to read you a few paragraphs from a column in an old issue of the *Tribune*. Then I want you to tell me what section of the paper I was reading."

"Like from the comics or the want ads?" I asked.

"Yes, something like that," Kayne said. "Ready? Listen closely:

The man was traveling quickly on the path home. Suddenly, he saw a man in a mask with something in his hand. When the man on the path saw what the man with the mask was holding, he turned and ran the opposite direction.

But then the man on the path saw a man coming toward him from the opposite direction, with the same object in his hand. The man on the path had to make a choice.

He felt his only chance was to run toward the man with the mask, knock him down and perhaps jar the object from his hand. He tried to do so, but he didn't succeed.

"Bill," Kayne asked, "what section of the paper was this from?"

My first thought was that this puzzle was too easy. He must be reading something from the police blotter, the part of the paper that reports on crimes that take place during the week. The guy must have been robbed by an armed masked man on his way to his house.

Then I thought, maybe the story was from the entertainment section. Maybe the man on the path and the man with the mask were characters in a movie or

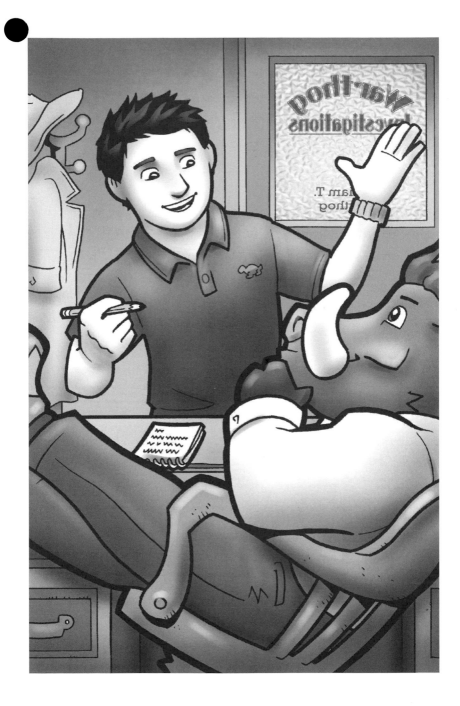

TV show. Or a book or a play. I couldn't decide between those options, so I was glad Bill was answering Kayne, not me.

I looked at Bill, who had a big smile on his face. (You have to know Bill a while to tell a smile from just ordinary tuskiness.)

"Do you know, Bill? Because if you don't, I'm going to have to find another detective," Kayne said.

"Of course I know," Bill said. "It was from the sports section."

"Very good," said Kayne Foster. "I think you'll do. Where did you get your smarts?"

"What I hope to have is wisdom," Bill answered, "and there is one book that can help you find that better than any other."

Bill and I went with Kayne to the *Tribune* building to negotiate a contract.

I knew there were three things I would have to ask Bill on the way home:

How did he guess the sports section?

What was this book he was talking about?

How much was Kayne going to pay him?

☞ **Turn to page 90 to find out!**

Chapter 2

The Case of the Were-cat

Bill and I figured it was only a matter of time before Kayne would ask us to investigate a story that Chris Franklin brought to him.

Chris was the neighborhood bully, and he was always scheming to make a buck or two by tricking other kids. How could he resist a chance to scheme for thousands of dollars?

Anyway, Kayne asked us to come to his office at the *Weekly Tribune,* where he handed us an envelope he had received in the mail from Chris. The most interesting thing in the envelope was a photograph.

"You don't believe that this photo is legitimate, do you, Kayne?" Bill asked.

It was a pretty amazing picture. It showed someone, or something, wearing a shirt and pants and shoes and a watch, but with a face and hands covered with lots of hair. It had catlike ears, fangs and claws.

The weirdest thing was that Chris had written under the photo that this was a picture of himself.

"I don't know if the picture is legitimate or not," Kayne said. "That's why I want you to investigate it. I would have dismissed the idea of a cat-person out of hand if I hadn't met a warthog detective. Please, read this letter that Chris Franklin sent with the picture."

Bill read the letter, and then he gave it to me to read. Here, you can read it for yourself:

Dear Mr. Foster,

You can end your search for the most bizarre story. That story is now in your hands.

This story begins two weeks ago on a dark and stormy night. I looked out the window to my backyard to check on my dog, Mr. Happyface, who should have been chained to his doghouse. (I named the dog when I was little, OK, so if you don't include his name in the newspaper story, I would appreciate it.)

Anyway, when I looked out, Mr. Happyface

was gone. I went out and found his collar. It looked like the collar had been torn by some huge claw. I saw tracks that went into the woods behind my house.

Some of the tracks were Mr. Happyface's, but some were huge tracks, like a cat's. I thought a mountain lion  must have made them. So I decided to look for Mr. Happyface. I grabbed a flashlight from the house and went into the woods.

After a few minutes, I could hear my dog's bark. I followed the tracks and sounds. Then I saw the strangest, most horrible sight.

Mr. Happyface was trapped in a hollow log, and outside of the log was a huge, weird creature. It didn't look quite like a man or quite like a big cat, but more like both combined.

I had to save Mr. Happyface.

I yelled and hit the creature with my flashlight. It turned and scratched me and bit my leg. Mr. Happyface came out and bit the thing's tail, and it went running off in the woods. Mr. Happyface and I went home.

Since that night, I have felt strange. When I pass cats on the street, I know it's weird, but I want to meow at them. All I want to eat is tuna.

The strangest thing happened when I went to the pet store to get dog food for Mr. Happyface. There was catnip on a shelf in the store. I stopped, picked some up and sniffed it. I wanted to eat the catnip, right then, but instead I bought a bag and brought it home.

When I got home, I ate the catnip and – as you can see in the picture – I transformed into a giant cat. After a few hours, I returned to my normal form.

I know this sounds too incredible, but if you doubt it, my father, Hal Franklin, filmed my transformation. Feel free to come and see the video at my house. Bring along the $50,000.

Sincerely,

Chris Franklin

"Come on, Nick," Bill said. "There is a video we need to view."

Kayne didn't come with us; he said he had to take care of some newspaper business.

"What are you doing here, Pumba and Timon?"

Chris said, when we knocked on his door. He didn't seem happy to see us.

"As I always seem to need to explain to you, our names are Bill and Nick. We're here as representatives of the *Weekly Tribune* to check out your story for the contest. I believe you have a video to show us."

Chris grumbled as he started the video.

On the screen, we saw Chris sitting on a couch, the same couch we were all sitting on. In the video, Chris was wearing the same clothes as in the photograph.

We watched as hair grew on his face and hands. His ears and teeth grew and claws began to sprout from his hands. It was bizarre. I wondered if the $50,000 was Chris's for the taking.

"Can we get out of here, now?" I whispered to Bill. "He might have more catnip. I don't want to be around when he transforms into that were-cat thing again."

"There was no real transformation," Bill said. "Didn't you watch?"

"Of course I watched," I said.

"But did you watch the watch?" Bill said. He turned to Chris. "Can I talk to you and your father?"

Bill talked with Chris and his father Hal Franklin in another room. I couldn't hear much, but I could hear

the words "liar" and "fraud" and then we left.

Bill and I talked on the way back to his office.

"I was kind of scared watching that video," I said, "though I know it's stupid to be afraid."

"Being afraid isn't necessarily stupid. As a matter of fact, fear of the right thing is the beginning of wisdom. That's what a wise man once said."

This puzzled me as much as how Bill figured out Chris's story was a fraud. Fortunately, Bill explained both on the walk back to the *Weekly Tribune* and Kayne's office.

How did Bill know from watching the video that Chris's story was a fraud?

What did Bill mean when he said fear of the right thing is the beginning of wisdom?

☞ Turn to page 92 to find out!

Chapter 3

The Case of the Iron Robot

I know most people have people for friends, as I do, but most people don't get to have warthogs for friends – so I feel fortunate.

Many people have furry friends, such as dogs, or even ferrets. (Some people consider their cats friends, but do the cats consider their people friends? I have my doubts.)

When Brad Tweety told the *Weekly Tribune* he had a metal friend, Kayne Foster asked Bill to investigate.

"He claims he can import cheap robots," Kayne told Bill. "He says that they're able to do much more than anything available before. He's trying to claim the prize for an unusual story, so I want you to check it out."

Brad's house turned out to be close to mine, and we arranged to meet in his garage. I hadn't met Brad before. He was in junior high, so he was a couple of years older than me, but he wasn't any taller.

"Good to meet you, Brad," Bill said. "I understand you have something unusual to show us."

"I certainly do. I hope I can trust you to keep this quiet until the story comes out in the paper. There's going to be such a demand for this new robot that I'll need all the time I can get to prepare," Brad said.

"It can't be that big a deal," I said. "No offense, but every toy and electronics store sells robots. I got a remote control monkey robot myself a couple years ago."

"That's the thing," Brad said. "You need to use a remote control. With Dudley, you need nothing of the kind. Come on out, Dudley!"

The door from the house opened, and down the stairs into the garage walked a little metal man. (It was not tiny, just little, about four and a half feet tall). Its light bulb eyes were flashing. I thought it had a tail, but then I saw the robot was trailing an extension cord that led back into the house.

The robot's chest was covered with buttons, and

some of the buttons were flashing lights. It had legs and arms, and everything was metal.

"Hello, I am Dudley," the creature said, with a mechanical voice. It walked up to me and held up its right hand for me to shake. I did. Its hand was cold.

"So this is a voice activated machine?" Bill asked.

"Yes, it responds to the voice it is programmed to obey. Dudley obeys me. It does whatever I tell it to do and agrees with everything I say."

I decided to try this feature out. "Dudley," I said, "touch your toes."

Dudley stood still.

"Dudley," Brad said with a grin, "touch your toes."

Dudley bent and touched its toes.

"You can talk with it?" I asked.

"Of course," Brad answered. "Say, Dudley, who's your buddy?"

"You are, Brad," the little tin man said.

"And am I right, that I am the coolest dude, ever?"

"Absolutely, Brad, you are the coolest dude, ever."

"That's quite a sunny day outside, isn't it Dudley?"

"Yes, such a sunny day," Dudley responded.

"Actually, there is a fierce storm raging, with

raining, lightning and thunder," Brad said.

"Horrible weather outside," Dudley said. "Awful."

"With Dudley, I'm never wrong. This robot is the best friend in the world," Brad said.

"Did you make Dudley?" Bill asked.

"No, it's a prototype of a robot manufactured in Poland. In Eastern Europe they have technology from the old Soviet Union. I have a cousin who works at the factory, and he sent it to me."

"Were any modifications made to the robot before your cousin sent it here?"

"Nope, none at all," Brad said. "Dudley is right off the assembly lines. It was made for the European market, and the company will be releasing robots there in a few months. After mine was shipped here, I just plugged it into the wall, and I had a mechanical friend. I expect I'll be the distributor for this product in the United States."

"What's it made of?" I asked.

"I think it's all iron on the outside, but obviously the inside is all electronic," Brad said.

"So, do you have it do chores?" I asked.

"Of course," Brad said. "Dudley, go to the driveway and bring the newspaper back to me."

Dudley began to do the task, but halfway down the driveway, its extension cord went taut.

"I'll have to re-plug its cord," Brad said.

Brad went in the house and unplugged the cord. Dudley's lights went off. Brad plugged the cord into a garage outlet. Dudley's lights went back on, and it fetched the paper.

"Good job getting the paper, Dudley!"

"Good job sending me for the paper," Dudley responded.

"I think we've seen enough," Bill said.

Brad looked excited. "So obviously you're pretty impressed with Dudley. The *Weekly Tribune* will put Dudley on the front page, right? I'm thinking of using the $50,000 to import more robots from Poland."

"I wouldn't get my hopes up," Bill said.

Bill and I began the walk to the *Weekly Tribune*.

"That was pretty impressive," I said.

"Yes, a fairly impressive fraud," Bill said.

"Huh?" I said.

"Do you know kids that could fit into a robot suit that size?"

"Sure, lots of kids," I said. "Do you mean—?"

"Yes," Bill said. "There may well be robots

available some day, but Dudley wasn't real. It was just a kid in an iron suit."

"How do you know?" I asked.

"Because Dudley didn't have the power to do the things it did," Bill said.

"Oh," I said. "Still, it would be cool to have someone who always agrees with you."

"I'm not sure about that," Bill said. "I think it is better to have another kind of iron friend."

"Huh?" I said again. I was not at the top of my talk game that day.

"No better friend than the proverbial friend who sharpens iron with iron."

"So no metal friends for me," I said. "I'll just stick with my tusked friend."

"Glad to hear it," Bill said.

How did Bill know Dudley wasn't a real robot?

What did Bill mean with all this talk about a proverbial iron friend?

☞ Turn to page 94 to find out!

Chapter 4

The Case of the Ant Slaves

I was surprised to see Bill reading about ants, outside of a cookbook.

Bill did talk about ants a lot. He would talk about how he enjoyed chocolate covered ants for dessert, ants sprinkled over salad, anty-pasta, etc. He was reading a scientific-looking book on ants, though, and that made me curious.

"Are you reading that for a case?" I asked.

"Yes, we'll be checking out another story for the *Weekly Tribune* bizarre news contest. We're going to the abandoned Excel toy factory on the edge of town."

Excel Toys had built a factory to manufacture Mr. Broccoli Head dolls, but another toy maker sued them and they ended up closing the factory. On the way to the factory, I asked Bill about the case.

"There is a kid by the name of Adam Plant who says he has come up with an amazing labor saving device," Bill explained.

"And this has something to do with ants?" I asked.

"We'll see," Bill said.

The factory had a large parking lot in front. There were no cars, just one bike in the bike rack. Bill knocked on a large, steel door.

The door rolled up into the wall, and out of the factory came a kid about my age, with blond hair. He was putting on a white lab coat, and he introduced himself as Adam Plant.

"You're really a warthog, aren't you?" Adam asked.

Bill nodded.

"You're not coming in," Adam said.

"Why's that?" I asked.

"I saw a nature special on TV the other night, and it showed a warthog living in an anteater's burrow. If a warthog will share an anteater's home, perhaps it shares an anteater's diet."

"You are suggesting that because I'm a warthog, I eat ants?" Bill said. "Yes, of course, I do eat ants, but

you don't have to worry about that, because I'm a professional. And if you don't let me in, Kayne Foster and the *Weekly Tribune* certainly will not be awarding you the $50,000 prize."

"What is it, exactly, we'll be looking at?" I asked.

"My ants," Adam said.

He led us down a long hallway and stopped by a glass window that looked into a room. The window had one-way glass, like the kind you see on TV shows where the police can look at suspects being interviewed. We saw ants inside the room, and also the parts for a Mr. Broccoli Head figure: the broccoli head-body, nose, mouth, eyes, hat and the rest.

As we watched, the pieces seemed to come together by themselves. The nose, mouth, mustache, all the pieces were being attached all by themselves.

"What's doing that?" I asked.

Adam laughed, "Why my ants, of course. Through special olfactory training, I've taught the ants to do simple chores, such as putting this toy together."

"Old factory training?" I was puzzled.

"Olfactory," Bill said. "He means he has been using scent clues, teaching the ants to do tasks by the sense of smell. It is possible."

We walked to another window and saw a room that looked like a kid's bedroom, complete with clothes and papers on the floor. The clothes seemed to be moving toward the dresser drawers and the papers toward the waste can on their own.

"The ants are doing that?" I asked.

"Of course," Adam said. "You can't see them very well because I trained the small, young ants and I needed to use dim light for these experiments."

"It'd be cool if I had ants to clean my room," I said.

"That's the idea," Adam said. "With the reward money from the *Weekly Tribune*, I'll be able to finish my ant breeding and training experiments. Pretty soon I'll have a much greater fortune from selling service ant teams around the world."

We looked inside one last room. In the room there were bottles and cups, many of the bottles marked with skulls and crossbones. Two of the bottles seemed to be pouring their contents into a beaker by themselves.

"There is no danger to humans from this dangerous chemical experiment, because the whole procedure is being conducted by ants."

"I wouldn't suppose I could go into the rooms to look at the ants more closely?" Bill asked.

"I'm afraid not," Adam said. "I can't imagine how a creature like you might panic them. One look at you could set their training back weeks or months."

"I would expect you to say that if your story was legitimate," Bill said. "You would say the very same thing, however, if your story was false and those demonstrations you said were done by ants were actually illusions created with dim lights, pulleys and fishing line."

"No need to worry that the demonstrations are illusions. I've been studying ants for years for this very purpose," Adam said.

"What breed of ants did you use?" I asked.

"That's a good question," Adam said. "There are a dozen different breeds of ants in the world, such as army ants, wood ants and farm ants. The ants you see here are worker ants."

"Very cool," I said, "and appropriate, because I think all the work at my home will soon be done by ants. More video game time is on the way."

"Don't count your video game hours before they're hatched or played or whatever, Nick. Adam has shown us that he isn't an expert on ants at all. Therefore his story is a fraud."

"What makes you say that?" Adam said.

Bill whispered in Adam's ear, and Adam said, "Oh."

Bill told Adam, "Take some time to really study ants, as a wise man once suggested. I think that wouldn't hurt you either, Nick. As for me, I'll go and study some ants, mixed with garlic and pesto sauce, and their effect on satisfying my hunger."

How did Bill know that Adam wasn't an ant expert? And what good can be found studying ants?

☞ Turn to page 96 to find out!

Chapter 5

Phil the Warthog Vs. Sprock's Brain Stuffer

It was nice to see Mike Green come into Bill's office, because I was pretty sure he wasn't looking to collect on the $50,000. Turned out he was interested in getting something else from Kayne Foster and the *Weekly Tribune*.

"Bill, Nick," Mike said, "I hear you have some connections with the *Tribune*, true?"

"Of a kind," Bill said. "Why do you ask?"

"I've noticed they don't have one of the most important features a newspaper should have, comics. I want to help them out by supplying them with a weekly *Phil the Warthog* comic."

Phil the Warthog, in Mike's comics, is a warthog

genetically engineered by a mad scientist to be intelligent and strong, who escaped to work as an agent for the government.

Mike is my age and he sells his *Phil the Warthog* comics to kids at school. He always shows the comics to Bill first. I suspect that's because Phil is based on Bill.

"Did you adapt one of your comic books into comic strip format for the *Tribune*?" Bill asked.

"I came up with a new story. Would you mind reading it and letting me know what you think?"

Instead of comic books, Mike had brought poster boards with four weeks' worth of *Phil* comics. The panel of the first comic showed Phil in the office of his boss, Shady Thompkins.

SHADY: I'm concerned, Phil. I believe that Dr. Werner Von Doomcough has been working with another mad, criminal scientist – Mr. Leonard Sprock.

PHIL: Sprock? The expert in brain enhancements?

SHADY: One and the same. There have been more thefts from zoos, and I suspect Dr. Doomcough is responsible.

PHIL: What animals have been abducted?

SHADY: A fruit bat, a Marion's tortoise, a Bengal tiger, an ostrich and a chicken.

PHIL: I'll get on the case, chief.

That was pretty much it for the first comic. The next one had Phil breaking into Doomcough's labs. Wordless panels showed Phil studying the machinery and coming across Sprock's brain stuffing machine. Then Phil found a filing cabinet and began to rifle through files labeled "Sprock's Brain Project."

It got a little more exciting then, as Phil was surprised by Doomcough's genetically engineered rhinoceros guards. Fortunately for Phil, these guards obviously had not been subjects of Sprock's brain stuffing machine.

Phil tricked the two guards into charging just as he opened a closet door and dived out of the way. The rhinos tried to turn, but they were too late. They were in the closet, and Phil had the door slammed closed and locked.

Phil headed out into the hallway and found himself facing Dr. Doomcough and Mr. Sprock. They had laser guns in their hands, pointing right at Phil.

"Well, the action is picking up," I said to Mike. "Let's see the next installment."

The strip showed Phil with all four legs tied against

a wall. Doomcough and Sprock stood nearby.

DOOMCOUGH: So, Phil, we finally meet again. I never understood why you left me.

PHIL: I left you, Doomcough, because your plans were evil. You are always trying to hurt others. And frankly, I also left because there is this funky smell around here.

DOOMCOUGH: Yes, about that. I've tried various air fresheners, but . . . Never mind that! My plan for world domination is almost complete.

PHIL: What is your plan?

DOOMCOUGH: Well, I might as well tell you, since you won't live to see my plan fulfilled.

PHIL: Why is that? Is it going to take, like, centuries?

DOOMCOUGH: No, my porky friend, because I will soon leave this room with Mr. Sprock, and then this room will fill with Jell-O. You will drown in Jell-O.

PHIL: Strawberry Jell-O?

DOOMCOUGH: Lemon.

PHIL: No!

DOOMCOUGH: So, it won't hurt to tell you my plan. You see, Mr. Sprock's brain stuffing machine has already stuffed specialized knowledge into five different animals.

PHIL: How exactly will that help with the world domination thing?

DOOMCOUGH: You fool, isn't it obvious? The animals will go on television game shows and use their vast knowledge to win huge amounts of money. That money will finance political campaigns, in which the mutated animals will run for office.

PHIL: And then?

DOOMCOUGH: Then, once in office, my animals will appoint me to important commissions, and I will use that power to get approval for subdivisions and then build giant shopping malls and then . . .

SPROCK: I thought we were going to use the money to build a giant weapon that we would use to threaten world governments unless we were put in power.

DOOMCOUGH: Yes, that would be quicker. We might go with that. But for now we'll leave you, Phil, to your Jell-O-y doom.

I dove for the new board, as I was anxious to get to the next installment.

Phil was alone in the room as the lemon Jell-O began to fill it. Fortunately, Doomcough had forgotten about Phil's tusks. He used them to cut the ropes and escaped back to Shady Thompkins' office.

SHADY: That is quite the evil plan Doomcough has underway. We must find a way to stop it. If only we knew the specific knowledge each animal had!

PHIL: I might be able to help there. I learned some things from Sprock's files.

SHADY: Did he use the tortoise, tiger, bat, ostrich and chicken?

PHIL: Yes, and each had a brain stuffed with a specific area of information. One with science, one with philosophy, one with literature, one with history and one with math.

SHADY: Did you find out which animal had which kind of knowledge? We must know.

PHIL: Not in so many words, but I have clues. The notes said the heaviest animal was to be given the weighty issues of philosophy.

SHADY: Anything else?

PHIL: Yes, the one that could live longest was to be given history, the tallest given literature, and a furry one given science. Is that enough?

SHADY: It'll have to be. You know that Doomcough may have found a way to get knowledge, but he still doesn't have wisdom.

And that's as far as the adventure went.

Bill said to Mike, "Well, the story is interesting. Preposterous as usual, but interesting. Nick and I will take it to Kayne and he can decide if he has a place for your comic strip in the *Weekly Tribune*."

"I want to read the rest of the story," I said. "I want to find out which animal has which kind of knowledge."

"That's obvious," Bill said. "Unfortunately, Shady's remark about knowledge and wisdom is not obvious enough to many people."

Do you know which animal had which kind of knowledge? And what is the difference between knowledge and wisdom?

☞ **Turn to page 98 to find out!**

Chapter 6

The Case of the Bogus Basketball Star

It was strange to see Bill wearing basketball shorts and a basketball jersey. I think warthogs lead the animal kingdom in knobbliness of knees. Bill had agreed to play on my neighborhood team that afternoon.

We were short a player since one of the guys on our team, Randy "Spills" Kibit, couldn't play. He accidentally sat on his dog, and his dog bit his, um, seat. Since Spills usually was the bench warmer, we needed a sub.

We were playing across town at Bryant Coldbee's house. He said he had a cool new court he had built himself. So the guys on my team (Joel, Blake, Luis and

Mark) met Bill and me at the elementary school, and we biked over to Bryant's house.

Bryant and his team were out in front of his house, and we shook hands all around. We went straight to Bryant's backyard. He did have a basketball court, but it was different from any I had seen before.

The court was cement, and that I was used to. But the lines were drawn with chalk, instead of paint. The really weird thing was the baskets. They were made of wood, instead of metal.

There were no nets on the baskets. They were real baskets, like wooden garbage cans or something.

We were all staring at the baskets, and Blake asked the question we were all thinking, "What's the deal with the baskets, Bryant?"

"I thought you'd never ask," Bryant said. "I've been researching the origins of basketball and the design done by the game's inventor, Dr. James Naismith. This court is set up the way a basketball court was originally meant to be."

"How do you get the ball out the basket?" Luis asked him.

"I wondered about that when I built the court. Took a while to figure out the hoops," Bryant said. "I

have this stick here to knock the ball out of the basket." There were small holes in the bottoms of the baskets that the stick could fit through.

It was time to play, so Bryant flipped a coin to see who would take which basket (a Naismith tradition, Bryant said).

The game did not go well for us Elm Streeters. It seemed every loose ball rolled to their side of the court. Every shot seemed to go in for their team, but for our team, the ball always seemed to bounce out of the basket.

The really impressive thing was that a couple of players on their team were able to dunk the ball, and they didn't seem much taller than us.

Bill had been sitting on the bench the whole game. Mark looked pretty beat, so Bill went in for him.

Bill isn't a very good player, but he does throw a really interesting free throw shot. He lies on his back and uses all four hooves to toss the ball in. It's the best part of his game.

We still ended up losing by ten points.

Bryant said, "Well, hate to brag, but we're the best."

"The court had something to do with it," Bill said under his breath.

"What was that?" Bryant said.

"Would you mind if I examined the court with a tape measure and level?" Bill asked.

"What are you suggesting?" Bryant said.

"I'm not suggesting anything. My observations lead me to believe that if I use a level I will find that this court slopes toward your basket. Also, I believe we'll find your basket is not as high as our basket."

"What do you mean by 'my observations'? Anyone looking at this court can see that everything is fair. This court is incredibly authentic.

"In fact, I wouldn't be surprised if your friend with the newspaper would like to do a story about this court. It'd be a good story. A story about this court would probably be $50,000 good."

Bill nodded, "If there is a story, it will be a story of deception. You know, amusement parks and tourist sites, whose attractions claim to defy gravity, use landscaping to create an effect and fool the eye.

"Bryant, you have done a clever job with the landscaping here. You have bushes planted alongside the court to make everything look even. But I believe you have taller bushes near the tall basket and shorter bushes by the shorter basket. The tape measure and level will reveal all."

"There's no need to measure anything," Bryant said. "This court was built to honor basketball's founder, Dr. James Naismith of the YMCA. I wouldn't dishonor his name with that kind of trick.

"The integrity of this game is really important to me. Did you know my dribbling style is based on the style Naismith originated for the game? From my research, I believe I'm dribbling just as the good doctor dribbled in that first game in Springfield, Massachusetts."

"I'm going to get my tools," Bill said.

I followed him, and called out, "Bill, you don't really believe Bryant is cheating. You heard what he just said."

Bill turned around, "I know Bryant is cheating *because* of what he just said."

Bill proved with his level and tape measure that one basket was taller than the other and that the court wasn't on the level. We agreed to play again the next week on a neutral court.

"From now on," Bill told Bryant, "use level scales."

"Scales?" Bryant asked.

"Look up the proverb," Bill said, "while the rest of us go out and look up some tacos. Nick, mind if I snag some dandelions on the way for toppings?"

What did Bryant say that convinced Bill he wasn't being honest?

And what is the proverb about level scales?

☞Turn to page 100 to find out!

Chapter 7

The Case of the Giant Chicken

I was not happy to wake up that morning at 6:00 AM.

I usually get up at 7:00 AM. That gives me plenty of time to get dressed, have breakfast and bike or walk to school on time.

That particular morning, the sound of a crowing rooster woke me. This was weird. My family didn't keep chickens, and as far as I knew, there were no chickens in the neighborhood.

I covered my head and tried to go back to sleep, but couldn't so I got up. My mom was in the kitchen and my dad was already off to work. Since I had spare time, I asked my mom if I could play video games. She said no, but I could read, so I read for awhile, had breakfast and walked to school. As I walked, I wondered about that crowing sound that woke me up.

I got to school to find a lot of other kids wondering about the same thing. It seemed everyone had heard a rooster. There were some kids, though, that were saying they knew what had made the sound.

Steven Martinski said he knew. "I looked out the window and saw a giant chicken."

Jared Prentiss nodded, "Yeah, I saw the same thing, a giant chicken out the window. I got up to see what was happening when I heard the crowing. After about five minutes, the chicken vanished."

I didn't take them that seriously, though. Those two were always joking.

I took their story more seriously when I got a call from Bill after school. The *Weekly Tribune* was swamped with calls from people wanting to submit their story about the giant chicken to win the $50,000 prize. Bill had assured Kayne Foster that we would investigate.

Unfortunately, I couldn't help that day because my teacher had loaded on the homework. I told Bill I could help him the next day if there was still any case left to solve.

Turned out there was, even though Bill had already done a lot of work.

"Here's what I did yesterday and most of today," Bill said. "The reporters received calls from all over town about this phenomenal fowl. By following up the calls, I was able to pinpoint its probable location."

"You don't actually believe there's a giant chicken?" I asked.

"Many people claim to have seen the same thing," Bill said. "They saw something. I asked a friend at the utility company if there was an unusual upsurge in power usage when the giant chicken was sighted."

"Did you find out anything?"

"Fortunately, yes," Bill said. "A house at North and Cherry used an amazingly large amount of electrical power right around 6:00 yesterday morning. We are going to pay a visit to the Billings' household."

It didn't take long to get to the house. Bill rang the doorbell.

A guy, a teenager, answered the door.

"Excuse me, I know this is unusual . . ." Bill said.

"A walking pig at my door? You bet this is unusual," the guy said.

"Warthog, actually, but my species is not important

right now. My occupation is. I'm a detective, and my name is Bill. This is my assistant Nick."

"Pleasure to meet you, Bill and Nick. My name is

Cosby, Cosby Billings." We shook hands (and hooves), and then Cosby surprised me by saying, "Are you here about the giant chicken?"

"As a matter of fact, yes," Bill said. "Are you responsible for this phenomenon?"

"I sure am," Cosby said. "My dad helped me get some of the equipment, but it was my idea, and I did all the work. Come out to the backyard and see."

We went to the backyard and saw an electronic superstore's worth of technology. There were speakers, computers, smoke machines and some things that looked like searchlights.

"I use holographic technology," Cosby said, "to produce the image of the chicken. I project the hologram in the air on the fog I make with these machines. To make the noise of the chicken crowing, I modified equipment that used to be a town emergency siren."

"I appreciate your forthrightness about all of this,"

Bill said. "You are aware, aren't you, that I am working for Kayne Foster and the *Weekly Tribune*, and you have probably forfeited any possibility of winning the bizarre story contest?"

"What bizarre story contest?" Cosby asked.

"You didn't know about the $50,000 contest?" I asked. This surprised me almost as much as when he first admitted he made the giant chicken.

"No," said Cosby. "I wish now I'd read the *Weekly Tribune* more closely."

"Then, would you tell us why you have gone to such trouble?" Bill asked.

Cosby reached into his pocket and pulled out a flyer. "It was a publicity stunt for my new business."

Bill and I read the flyer.

Need a cheerful voice to wake you up in the morning? Nothing is more cheerful than the crow of a rooster! I'll provide you with one of nature's alarm clocks for a low, low price. You'll be up early every morning, and you'll get the bonus of eggs as well!

Cosby said, "I'm planning on treating the town to the giant chicken a couple more times this week, and then I'm going to blanket every neighborhood with

flyers so people can have a chicken of their own."

Bill shook his head. "Cosby, you need to look into the city noise ordinances before you try this stunt again. Also, before you do any more with this business, you're going to have to learn more about chickens and more about people."

"More about people?" Cosby asked.

"Yes, there is a proverb that reminds us that not everyone likes a cheerful voice in the morning. Now, about that flyer . . ."

Bill explained to Cosby why it might be best not to use that flyer, and told him where he could learn more about the city's noise and animal ordinances.

Many disappointed readers of the *Weekly Tribune* learned in its next issue that the giant chicken story was not going to make them $50,000.

What did Cosby still need to learn about chickens?

What did Cosby still need to learn about people?

☞ Turn to page 102 to find out!

Chapter 8

The Case of the Parental Hypnosis

Bill called me after Kayne Foster gave him another bizarre story to investigate. Bill filled me in on his conversation with Kayne.

"Someone called in with a story that he claimed could win the $50,000 incredible story prize. He claimed to have something that would change the lives of kids throughout the world. Kayne told me the caller said specifically that he did not want, in his words, 'that stupid pig snooper checking it out.'

"I asked Kayne what he said to that, and Kayne said he told the caller that you and I are doing fine investigating work, and anyone who wants to submit a story for the prize has to put up with our snooping."

I said to Bill, "May I play the detective and guess whose story we'll be checking out?"

"Certainly, Nick," Bill chuckled.

"Could it possibly be Chris Franklin?" I asked.

"Why Nick Sayga," Bill said, "you are developing great powers of deduction!"

Bill didn't hand out compliments like that too freely, so I took it. After checking with my mom, I headed off to meet Bill at Chris Franklin's house.

Chris met us at the door with his usual sneer, "Why if it isn't Pig-man and the Boy Blunder."

"A pleasure to see you as well, Chris," Bill said pleasantly. "Though I understand that you didn't wish Kayne to send us as his representatives."

"It doesn't matter," Chris said. "Even Mr. Happyface could tell you this discovery will win the *Weekly Tribune's* prize. You might as well come in."

Chris led us to his living room and told us to wait while he got his equipment and made a phone call.

He came back with three pairs of sunglasses and what looked like a really big flashlight.

"Is this the big story?"

"It sure is, Ten Toes Jam," Chris said. "This is the greatest hypnotic device ever created."

"Are you going to use it to put us under some kind of hypnotic trance?" Bill asked.

"No, of course not," Chris said. "In the first place, if I put you under a trance, you wouldn't be able to tell the *Weekly Tribune* that this is all true, because the trance makes you forget.

"In the second place, it doesn't work as well if you know I'm trying to put you under, because you would fight it. And in the third place, it didn't work on Mr. Happyface, so if it doesn't work on dogs, it probably doesn't work on even lower life forms such as yourself, warthog."

Bill smiled pleasantly and asked, "How *do* you expect us to verify your story?"

"That's why I made the phone call," Chris said. "My friend, Justin, is coming over to prove how incredible this device can be."

The doorbell rang, and Chris asked Bill to answer it and bring Justin in the room. ("Just so you'll know I'm not cluing him in on this all," Chris said.)

When Justin was in the room, Chris jammed one pair of sunglasses on his face and handed the others to Bill and me, saying, "Put these on, quick!"

We did, and just as Justin said, "Hey, how about a

pair for me?" there was a big flash from Chris's flashlight thing. Justin's face went blank. He was just staring straight forward. It was kind of weird.

"Justin is now under a deep hypnotic trance. He will not notice time passing or remember anything that happens except the instructions I give him.

"This is the world's greatest hypnotic device. After I win the *Weekly Tribune* prize money, I'll be able to market this device to kids around the world."

"Why to kids?" Bill asked.

"Can't you imagine the possibilities if kids were able to hypnotize their parents? Kids could make the rules at home. No more bedtimes or homework! Imagine the possibilities!" said Chris.

"I would like to have more than a half hour a day for video games," I muttered.

"Exactly," Chris said. "I'm sure you would pay to make that happen, too. Now watch me give Justin three commands. When he comes out of the trance, he'll follow these commands, and they are commands he would only obey if he were hypnotized."

Chris looked at Justin. "When you awaken, first,

you will talk about me as the greatest person ever!"

"It would take more than hypnosis to make me say that," I muttered, but Bill hushed me.

"Second," said Chris, "you will eat dog food and think it is ice cream, and third, you will bite Bill's tail."

"Excuse me!" Bill said.

"All right," Chris said. "You will make one attempt to bite Bill's tail." Chris flashed the device again.

"Hey, Chris," Justin said, "I'm really glad you invited me over here. I've been wanting to tell you you're the greatest, so smart, nice and good looking, and the way you beat up on little kids is so cool . . ."

"That's enough, Justin," Chris said. "Would you like some ice cream?"

"Sure," Justin said.

Chris led us to the kitchen and served Justin a bowl of Liver-flavored Healthy Chunks for Chubby Dogs.

"Yes!" Justin said. "Chocolate chip cookie dough, my favorite!" and he grinned as he began to eat the dog food.

Bill crossed the room to examine the dog food can. When Justin saw Bill's tail, Justin dove for it. Bill swooshed his tail away just in time, and Justin went back to his ice cream.

"So what do you think?" Chris asked.

"I'm impressed," I said.

"You put on quite a show," Bill said.

"This isn't just a show," Chris said. "Kids can use my device to hypnotize their parents and get away with anything."

"You could convince them you're doing homework while you're really playing video games," I said.

"You could play for hours," Justin told me, "instead of half an hour. I can't believe parents are so strict, I mean . . ."

"As I said," Bill interrupted, "this is a nice show, but this is obviously a fraud. You've got to learn, Chris, the discipline of your parents is more valuable than even the *Weekly Tribune's* prize money."

"Bill, are you going to explain what went on here on the way back to your office?" I asked.

"As always," said Bill.

How did Bill know the hypnotic device was a fraud? And what's so great about parental discipline?

☞ Turn to page 104 to find out!

Chapter 9

Bill and the Wise Dreams

I've often told Bill to be more careful choosing his snacks after dinner. Otherwise he has weird dreams. He told me about a wild one he had the other night.

"I know, I know," Bill said. "I shouldn't have had that cricket-topped chocolate sundae with orange soda just before bed the other night. At the start of my dream, I thought I was having a nightmare, but I wasn't."

"Why did you think it was a nightmare?" I asked.

"Because the first thing I saw was a soldier holding a sword over a little baby."

"The soldier was going to kill a little baby?" I asked. "What kind of soldier was that?"

"He was dressed in a robe," Bill said. "I realized it

was Old Testament times, so I had an idea of what was happening. As the sword was raised, a woman cried out and said something in Hebrew.

"Then a man called out. I saw it was a king. He said something in Hebrew and the soldier lowered his sword. The king then spoke to the two women standing there, and the woman who had cried out was given the baby."

"So was the whole dream in Hebrew? I wonder if the food you eat is related to the language you dream in. Like if you eat grub pizza you'd dream in Italian. Spanish would go with beetle tacos. I don't see what orange soda and a cricket sundae has to do with Hebrew though, so never mind. Isn't it dull to dream in a foreign language?" I asked.

"It would have been," Bill said, "but you know how dreams can be. Suddenly, I could speak Hebrew. Or everyone else could speak English. Anyway, I could understand people.

"And I knew I had to speak to the king."

"Did you know who the king was?" I asked.

"I was pretty sure," Bill said. "To be certain, I asked the soldier, 'Is that King Solomon?'

"'It is,' he said. 'Now who, or what, are you?'

"I thought for a moment, and then said, 'Your king thirsts for knowledge, and surely he would like to meet an odd creature like me.' The soldier agreed, and brought me to the king.

"The king asked who I was. I told him, 'My name is Bill, and I am a warthog. I know this is strange, to see a talking creature like myself, but believe me, it is just as strange to find myself thousands of years before my time talking to the king of Israel.'

"King Solomon looked at me and said, 'So how would you explain these strange things?'

"I responded honestly, 'The only explanation I can think of is that this is just a dream. Since I'm here, could you tell me why that soldier was about the kill the baby?'

"The king looked very serious. 'The baby was never in danger, but I wanted those women to believe he was.'

"I asked why.

"King Solomon smiled grimly, 'The two women came with the baby to my throne looking for justice. Each woman claimed the baby as her own. They lived in the same house and had both given birth to a son within days of each other. One of the babies had died.'

"I remembered this story, but I asked anyway, 'So how could you know which woman was telling you the truth?'

"The king said, 'I told the women I would cut the

 baby in half and give each woman half a child. I trusted the real mother would not let such a thing happen.'

"I had seen that his plan had worked. 'How did you get such wisdom?' I asked.

"'Believe it or not,' the king said, 'I got the wisdom in a dream. In this dream, the Lord came to me and told me to ask for whatever I wanted. I asked for wisdom. God has often worked this way. He spoke to our fathers Abraham and Jacob in dreams.'

"I nodded. The king went on, 'After that night, I found that God had given me wisdom to rule this kingdom. It was more than a dream.'

"Solomon and I talked for a long time. He asked about our time and the life of a warthog and a detective. I told him about how a detective, like a king, needs great wisdom to do his job well.

"I didn't tell Solomon about my dreams. Sure, I have dreamed about Moses the Lawgiver, an opossum accused of murder, and now about a king of Israel. Most of my dreams are about yummy insects and vegetation, though, and I didn't think he would be interested.

"Solomon told me about a dream his father David had. King David's dream was to build a temple to honor God, but David could not, so he left the dream for Solomon.

"Solomon then talked to me about his nation's dream of a Messiah that would come to save Israel from sin and bless all nations.

"Being from the future let me to tell Solomon something about how that dream came true.

"I asked the king how he came to write the book of Proverbs. He said he hadn't written such a book, but that it was a great idea, and he would get right on it.

"We talked again about how one of us was definitely dreaming, because this couldn't really be happening. Then he asked if I wanted to take a little test – a story about a dream.

"King Solomon said, 'A man told me about his brother who was killed by a dream. The brother dreamed he was climbing to the top of Mount Sinai. He finally reached the top of the mountain.'

"Solomon went on, 'When he reached the top, he looked over a cliff, was startled and fell and fell and fell. He died of fright instantly during the dream.'

"I said to Solomon, 'Did you tell the storyteller you knew he was lying about his brother's dream?'

"'I did,' he said.

"Solomon and I both laughed, and then I woke up."

I asked Bill how much of the dream about King Solomon was true, and he told me where to look it up. Then I asked him how he and King Solomon knew the man was lying about his brother's death, and Bill just laughed.

I think Bill is wiser when he's asleep than I am when I'm awake. Of course, I'm smart enough not to mix chocolate sundaes, crickets and orange soda.

How did Solomon and Bill know the man was lying about his brother's dream? And where can you find out about King Solomon?

☞ Turn to page 106 to find out!

The Case of the
Little Purple Person

"Nick, it would be unethical," Bill was arguing.

"Hey, they're looking for an unusual story," I argued back. "No offense, but in the dictionary your picture is right next to the definition of unusual."

I was at Bill's office, and we had been going back and forth like this for a while. I had finally realized the best bizarre story for the *Weekly Tribune* would be one about a warthog detective.

Bill said it wouldn't be right to submit a story for the contest since we had been given the responsibility to check out each story.

"Bill," I said, "why don't we just approach Kayne Foster and let him decide if he can accept the story?"

Just then, there was a knock on Bill's door. I opened it and was amazed to see Kayne himself.

"Kayne," I said, "what a coincidence! We were just going to tell you we know what your prize-winning story should be!"

Kayne looked puzzled. "You've heard about the alien from outer space?"

"No, we haven't," Bill said. "Never mind Nick's story; tell us yours."

Kayne launched in, "We got a scoop at the *Tribune* today from a reader who said he had top secret information. He would give us an exclusive if we published the story within the next two days, and after that he would have to go to the federal government.

"I agreed to meet the source at his home. I did, and what can I tell you? How could there be a bigger story than an alien from across the galaxy? My reporter's instinct told me to publish the story immediately, to be sure we'd have an exclusive for the *Weekly Tribune*.

"The only thing that stopped me was our agreement. I said I'd run all the stories past you. Let's head right over so you can OK the story."

I was surprised to see a car with a driver waiting for us outside Bill's office. Kayne said, "We need to

move quickly. Time is not on our side. Oh, I agreed, for security's sake, to call our source Mr. X."

We arrived at a house across town and knocked at the front door. A kid opened the door and Kayne said, "I'd like to introduce Mr. X."

I recognized the kid, Chase Pendergrass; he was in my soccer league. "Hey, Chase," I said.

"Nick! I wasn't expecting you. Sorry about Mr. X and the hush-hush stuff, but this is a big deal. I don't know why this space alien came to my house, but it did, just like the movie with the flying bikes.

"I'd like to introduce you to Grapey. First you'll have to wash up." Chase took us to his bathroom where he gave us surgical gowns to wear and antibacterial soap to put on our hands and faces. "I want to make sure Grapey doesn't get hurt by any Earth germs," Chase said.

"It's those little details that make me think we're onto something here," Kayne whispered to Bill.

We went into a room that was all white. A TV was playing there, with a metal canister next to it. A little person, wearing another surgical gown, sat in a wooden rocking chair.

I tried not to stare. The little person had purple skin, big pointy ears and huge metal shoes.

"Gentlemen," Chase said, "I'd like to introduce you to my guest, our planet's guest: Grapey from the planet Belzaar circling Alpha Centauri. Hello, Grapey!"

"Hello Earth people!" the creature said in a very high voice. Then the creature lifted one end of a hose connected to the canister and breathed from it.

"That's a helium tank," Chase said. "On Grapey's planet the atmosphere is all helium. I had to rent some helium tanks from the party supply store so Grapey could breathe. People usually use this stuff to blow up balloons."

"When did Grapey arrive on Earth, and why is it here?" Bill asked.

Grapey spoke in a very squeaky voice, "On our planet we have received your radio signals, and I came as an ambassador of our people. I observed you Earthers for several days before I decided to make first contact. I thought it would be safest to first contact one of your younglings.

"I feel safe enough now for you to let my presence be known through your papyrus communicators. Then I will meet with your government officials."

"And where is your vehicle?" Bill asked.

"Your people are not ready for our technology," Grapey said. "My vehicle is well hidden."

"Did Chase, or should I say Mr. X, provide you with your clothes?" Bill asked.

"Yes, we do not use clothes on our planet, so this creature provided me with these robings. The metal shoes were necessary, because otherwise my floating might startle your Earth eyes."

"What?" I said, wondering what this thing was talking about.

It looked at me and said, "As mentioned, on my planet we breathe helium, the galaxy's second most common element. As you know, helium causes balloons to float. If it were not for these heavy shoes, I would be floating as well."

"That must be quite an adjustment, coming to Earth," Bill said.

"Yes, on our planet, since we all breathe helium, no one thinks anything of floating from one place to another, but people are not used to such things in your world," Grapey said.

"Pretty incredible, huh?" Kayne said. "Do we have a tale to tell, or what?"

"Yes," Bill said. "A tall tale. Who is this person, Chase? Breathing helium is not good for us Earthers, and I hope you used a safe dye on this person's skin."

Bill talked quietly with Chase and Grapey (who was really Chase's cousin, Sarah, from out of state). Chase admitted the story was a fraud, concocted to collect the $50,000.

On the drive home, Kayne looked discouraged.

Bill tried to cheer him up, "It's good you found out, even for Chase's sake. As the proverb says, a fortune made from lies doesn't last. Another proverb says when you find a true story it will be worth the money."

"Will I ever find a story I can print?" Kayne moaned.

"About that . . ." I said.

How did Bill know Grapey wasn't really an alien? Did Kayne ever find a bizarre story for his contest? And Bill was talking about some proverbs – which proverbs were they?

☞ Turn to page 108 to find out!

The Case
of the
Newspaper Boy

Q: *How did Bill ever come up with the sports section of the paper?*

A: You have to think about what different meanings the words in the story might have. Bill realized the story was about baseball.

The "home" in the story was not a house, but home base. The man on the path was the runner. The man with the mask was the catcher with a baseball in his hand. The third man, the one who came at the runner from the opposite direction, was playing third base and had the runner caught in a rundown between third base and home. The runner tried to run for home and was tagged by the catcher.

Q: *Now what is this book of wisdom that Bill was talking about?*

A: You might be thinking the Bible, which is a good

guess. Bill was thinking about a particular book in the Bible, the book of Proverbs.

The book begins in this way, "The proverbs of

Solomon son of David, king of Israel: for attaining wisdom and discipline . . . let the discerning get guidance – for understanding proverbs and parables, the sayings and riddles of the wise."

Understanding riddles is Bill's business, but we all need help in dealing with life's everyday riddles.

And how much was Kayne going to pay Bill for investigating stories submitted to the *Tribune*?

Enough.

The Case of the Were-cat

Q: *What sort of tracks did Chris leave that proved he was no were-cat?*

A: Bill doubted Chris's story initially, because, well, frankly, it was Chris Franklin. And if you have read any of Bill's other books you would doubt Chris too.

After the video, Bill asked Nick if he had "watched the watch." The evidence was there.

Chris had made the video with his father using stop-motion photography. They would film Chris for a bit, then stop the camera and apply make-up. Then they would film again, repeating the process until Chris's were-cat transformation looked complete.

Bill suspected this was the method used, but he had proof from watching the watch Chris wore. The time on the watch would move suddenly forward again and again, proving the camera had stopped.

Q: *What was Bill talking about when he said, "Fear of the right thing is the beginning of wisdom"?*

A: Proverbs 1:7 says, "The fear of the Lord is the  beginning of knowledge."

Fear can be a good thing. A little kid should be afraid of a busy street and a hot stove. It shows the kid is starting to understand how the world works.

Once we start to understand God, it makes sense to be afraid of His power. God wants us to go from that fear to a real relationship with Him.

Of course, being afraid of were-cats – that might not be so bright.

The Case of the Iron Robot

Q: *Why did Bill pull the plug on Brad's entry in the bizarre story contest?*

A: It has to do with Bill's remark that Dudley didn't "have the power" to do what he did.

Brad claimed the robot was made in Poland, a European country, and that the robot was originally supposed to be used in Europe. Brad said no changes were made to the robot.

Yet, Dudley had a power cord that was plugged into the outlets in Brad's house. In Europe, the electrical power system is different. A European appliance needs an adapter to be used in the United States of America, just as American appliances need adapters to be used in Europe. Bill could see that Brad did not have an adapter on the end of the cord.

The power cord powered the light bulbs, not the

robot. Dudley was just Brad's little brother, Aidan, in a robot costume.

(Of course, if you were wondering how a Polish robot learned English so quickly, Bill might have been wondering that as well.)

Q: *Bill proved Dudley was a fake, so where is a real iron friend found?*

A: As for the iron business, Proverbs 27:17 reads, "As iron sharpens iron, so one man sharpens another."

 The idea here is that just like you sharpen a metal blade with another piece of metal, people can keep each other sharp.

You don't want to be around people that agree with you all the time. It's better to sharpen your mind with friends that challenge you, whether they are human or warthog.

The Case of the Ant Slaves

Q: *How could Bill know for sure that Adam was manufacturing lies, not Mr. Broccoli Head toys?*

A: Nick had asked Adam a question about the breed of ant Adam used, and the answer tipped off Bill. Two things proved to Bill that Adam wasn't an ant expert.

Adam had said, "There are a dozen breeds of ants in the world," when, in fact, there are almost 10,000 different types of ants in the world.

He also said that the breed of ant he used was a worker ant. Worker ants are not a breed. The name refers to a role, played within most species of ants.

Adam admitted he had used an automated system of fishing line and mechanical devices to make it look like ants were doing the work.

It was all a ruse to try to trick the *Weekly Tribune* out of the $50,000 prize.

Q: *What was Bill referring to when he talked about a wise man recommending ant study?*

A: Proverbs 6:6-8 reads, "Go to the ant, you sluggard [lazy person]; consider its ways and be wise! It has no

commander, no overseer or ruler, yet it stores its provisions in summer and gathers its food at harvest."

Adam needed to follow an ant's example of hard work rather than trying to cheat others out of their money.

Nick, too, could learn from an ant's example and gripe a little less about cleaning his room.

One can learn from ants, as well as warthogs.

Phil the Warthog Vs. Sprock's Brain Stuffer

Q: *Which animal knew what, and did Mike ever get his comic strip in the* Tribune?

A: Kayne did decide to put *Phil the Warthog* in the *Weekly Tribune*, and public response has been quite positive. (There's even talk about a *Phil the Warthog* book series, if you could imagine such a thing.)

Were you able to figure out which animal had which kind of knowledge?

The animal that can weigh the most is a Bengal tiger (up to 650 pounds), so it was given philosophy. The animal that can live the longest is a Marion's tortoise (which has been known to live over 150 years), so it got history. The tallest, the ostrich (a male ostrich can be 9 feet tall), went with literature. A tiger and a bat are both furry, but the tiger had a subject, so the bat went with science. That left math for the chicken.

Q: *What is the difference between wisdom and knowledge?*

A: Knowledge is knowing stuff. It's good to learn facts and figures and all. Wisdom is the ability to use knowledge to make good choices, which is even better.

The Case of the Bogus Basketball Star

Q: *How did Bill know the court was fouling up the basketball game?*

A: Bill was pretty sure there was something wrong with the court, even though Bryant said the court was properly built. Something Bryant told Bill assured him that Bryant was being intentionally dishonest.

Bryant said his dribbling style was based on the authentic style used when the game was first played.

Bill knew the original rules of basketball did not include dribbling. Dr. James Naismith originally created 13 rules for the game. Rule number three stated, "A player cannot run with the ball; the player must throw it from the spot he catches it, allowances to be made for a man who catches the ball when running if he tries to stop."

Bryant admitted he really hadn't studied the

origins of the game closely. He just wanted to make a court on which his team could win.

Q: *What does a proverb about scales have to do with any of this?*

A: Proverbs 11:1 says, "The Lord abhors [hates]  dishonest scales, but accurate weights are his delight."

Merchants who cheat people with crooked scales for sales make God mad. He is not pleased with any cheating, in business, sports or school.

We may not make basketball courts or use scales to sell things, but there are plenty of other areas where we need to be accurate and honest.

The Case of the Giant Chicken

Q: *How did Bill know that Cosby had a lot to learn about non-holographic chickens?*

A: Bill knew Cosby needed to learn about chickens because of what Cosby wrote on his flyer.

The flyer promised not only the rooster as an alarm clock, but the bonus of eggs. Bill knew from that, as you may well know, too, that Cosby had much to learn about chickens.

Roosters are male, of course, and they do most of the morning crowing. Male chickens do not lay eggs.

Cosby checked out the city noise ordinances. He found that his giant chicken sounds violated the noise ordinances, and that real roosters would as well.

According to the city livestock ordinances, however, a home could keep up to a dozen hens. Bill is now considering getting a couple for the fresh eggs.

Q: *Bill said that Cosby needed to read a certain proverb to learn about people. What was it?*

A: Now about that proverb: Proverbs 27:14 says, "If a man loudly blesses his neighbor early in the morning, it will be taken as a curse."

It's important to consider the feelings of others. Some people need time to wake up in the morning, or are sad for other reasons, and aren't ready for cheerfulness. We need to show consideration for the feelings of other people.

And, of course, the feelings of warthogs.

The Case of the Parental Hypnosis

Q: *Why wasn't Bill blinded by Chris's demonstration of the hypnosis device?*

A: Bill assumed Chris's hypnosis device was a fraud, because, well, it was Chris. He suspected Chris had set up Justin ahead of time to fake a hypnotic trance, but Bill needed a way to prove it.

The proof came when Justin made a comment about Nick's parents restricting him to a half hour of video gaming a day. Nick mentioned his video game restrictions while Justin was under his so-called trance. According to Chris, Justin wasn't supposed to remember what took place during the trance.

Q: *Why does Bill think discipline is so great?*

A: Bill had read what Proverbs says about the subject of parents and discipline.

Proverbs 13:24 reads, "He who spares the rod hates his son, but he who loves him is careful to discipline him." The proverb means that kids need

guidance, and one way that parents show love is through discipline.

Proverbs 3:11-12 makes clear that God shows love in the same way, "My son, do not despise the Lord's discipline and do not resent his rebuke, because the Lord disciplines those he loves, as a father the son he delights in."

It's hard to believe, but some day we'll be glad our parents kept us in line. It's a good line.

Bill and the Wise Dreams

Q: *How did Bill know right away why Solomon judged that the storyteller's dream was false?*

A: Though there is, of course, no way Bill could really meet King Solomon, he had read enough about the great man that he felt he knew him.

Bill knew that Solomon would easily see through a story such as the one the man told about the death of his brother, as you might well have. Solomon's judgment showed how well he knew the nature of dreams.

The man claimed that his brother died of fright during a dream about falling from a great height. This claim is an obvious lie for one simple reason. If the brother died during his dream, he would not have been able to tell the man or anyone else what he was dreaming about.

Q: *Can I get to know Solomon like Bill does, and will God ever ask me in a dream if I want something?*

A: To get to know King Solomon better yourself, you can read about him in the Bible. The book of

1 Kings, chapter 3 contains both the story of how Solomon gained wisdom from God and the story of the mothers who claimed the baby.

The dreams in which God spoke to Abraham and Jacob are in Genesis 15 and Genesis 28:10-17.

David's dream of building a temple for God is in 1 Chronicles 22. You can read in 1 Kings 5-8:13 about how Solomon made his father's dream real.

The dream of a coming Messiah is in many places in the Bible's Old Testament, in Isaiah 53 for example. Jesus Christ came to make that dream true (John 11:51-52), and you can read about Him in Matthew, Mark, Luke and John.

If you are ever wondering what you should ask God for, maybe it would be best to ask for wisdom first (even before that new video game system).

The Case of the Little Purple Person

Q: *How did Bill know that Grapey wasn't for real?*

A: The big clue had to do with helium. A helium-filled balloon floats because helium is lighter (less dense and heavy) than the air surrounding the balloon.

Grapey claimed creatures float on its planet because they breathe helium. However, if the planct's atmosphere was helium, then the creatures would not have a lighter substance inside them than the air surrounding them. Helium would be on the outside and on the inside, and so the creatures would not float.

Q: *And those proverbs Bill talked about?*

A: Other writers, along with Solomon, wrote parts of the book of Proverbs. Proverbs 21:6 reads, "A fortune made by a lying tongue is a fleeting vapor and a deadly snare." Lying to get something will never be worth it.

Proverbs 23:23 reads, "Buy the truth and do not sell it; get wisdom, discipline and understanding." The proverb writers assure us one of the most valuable things we can get is knowledge and wisdom, which can come from parents, school, church and (especially) God's Word.

Q: *Did Kayne and the* Weekly Tribune *ever find a winner?*

A: As a matter of fact, Nick wrote up and submitted the stories in this book. Kayne and the reporters on his newspaper staff all agreed that the adventures of a detective warthog were the most bizarre stories they had seen.

Bill insisted that he and Nick could not keep the prize money. Nick gave half of the money to his church, and Bill gave the other half to an organization that helps endangered species. Nick agreed it was the wise thing to do.

"Crime is like a cockroach, but not as tasty."
– Bill the Warthog

Test your detective skills alongside Bill and Nick in *Full Metal Trench Coat* and *Guarding the Tablets of Stone*!

LP48301
ISBN 10: 1-58411-068-6
ISBN 13: 978-1-58411-068-2

LP48302
ISBN 10: 1-58411-073-2
ISBN 13: 978-1-58411-073-6

Learn more about the large-toothed detective at:
www.legacyXpress.com